To a few little ones;
Matilda, Lila, Ajay and Noomi.
You're never fully dressed without a smile!
-Emily

Special thanks to Don G., Erin H., Hannah T.,
Kathleen Z., Nadeije A., Oliver O.,
Sarah K., Savanna D.,
my family and the internet
for all of your loving support.

To the Moon

Text copyright © 2014 by Emily A. Lovejoy
Illustrations copyright © 2014 by Emily A. Lovejoy
All rights reserved.

Book design by Emily A. Lovejoy and Matt Maghan

Printed in USA

ISBN 978-0615960807

To the Moon

written and illustrated
by Emily Lovejoy

The sun rose bright.
The warm breeze blew
the dandelion seeds
across the grass.

A young girl named
Lilith played outside,
humming the sweetest
tune that drifted with
the sounds of nature.

Lilith was a curious girl, always teaching herself new things. On this particular day she decided to find the moon. It was a mysterious thing she wanted to know more about. She had the perfect friend to help her get anywhere.

Lilith's friend was a little rabbit named Hopsi. Hopsi sprung out from her home in the ground with devotion to Lilith. Hopsi knew just what to do and how things should be done, always ready to complete any task.

The two little ones,
Lilith and Hopsi, set out
on their adventure to find
the moon. First, they came
upon a large patch of birch
trees.

High in the trees was a bird, named Chirp. Chirp hopped along branches collecting bugs and other such things. Hopsi asked, "Oh Chirp, since you seem to be closer to the moon high in the trees, could you tell us how to get there?"

Chirp replied, "Yes, I have a very wise friend at the edge of the forest. There you'll find Swift the fox. Where the trees meet the meadow, Swift, my friend will lead you to the moon. Sorry that I cannot help more, but my baby eggs are hatching."

Chirp also warned them
to be careful of the moon.
That didn't stop them, the
two little ones traveled on
their way.

Hopsi and Lilith set out to find Swift, jumping over fallen branches and weaving through the thick wooded forest. Finally, they made it to where the trees met the grassy plain.

There sat Swift, a small character with glowing orange fur. The fox moved towards the two little travelers and said, "What brings you two to my neck of the woods?"

Hopsi said, "To the moon, we're going to the moon! Chirp told us that you would lead us there. Will you help us?"

Swift replied, "Surely I cannot help you. I do not know how to find the moon. However, I do know who can help. The bees will help. They fly and travel so much that they must know how to get to the moon. Sorry I cannot help more, I'm nocturnal and it's way past my bedtime."

Swift also warned them to watch out for the moon, it may be sinister. That didn't stop them, the two little ones traveled on their way.

Lilith and Hopsi skipped into the meadow in search of the bees. They came across a large flower patch. The two adventure seekers stood quietly amongst the painted field of flowers. They could hear leaves rattling and blades of grass swishing together. It wasn't long before they heard the buzzing sound of bees.

Lilith, with her sweet soft voice said, "Oh bees, little honey bees, please come out and help."

Three little bees carrying loads of fluffy yellow pollen appeared and flew towards them.

The bees bopped up and down through the air. The smallest bumblebee said with a buzzy voice, "Happy to help! Bzz." The medium sized bee said, "I've never been. Bzz, but I know that you have to go up!" The largest bee said, "I suggest you start heading upwards. Bzz. You can get upwards by climbing the hill. Sorry we cannot help more, we must keep pollinating and making honey."

The three honeybees also warned them that the moon is a creature that prowls. That didn't stop them, the two little ones traveled on their way.

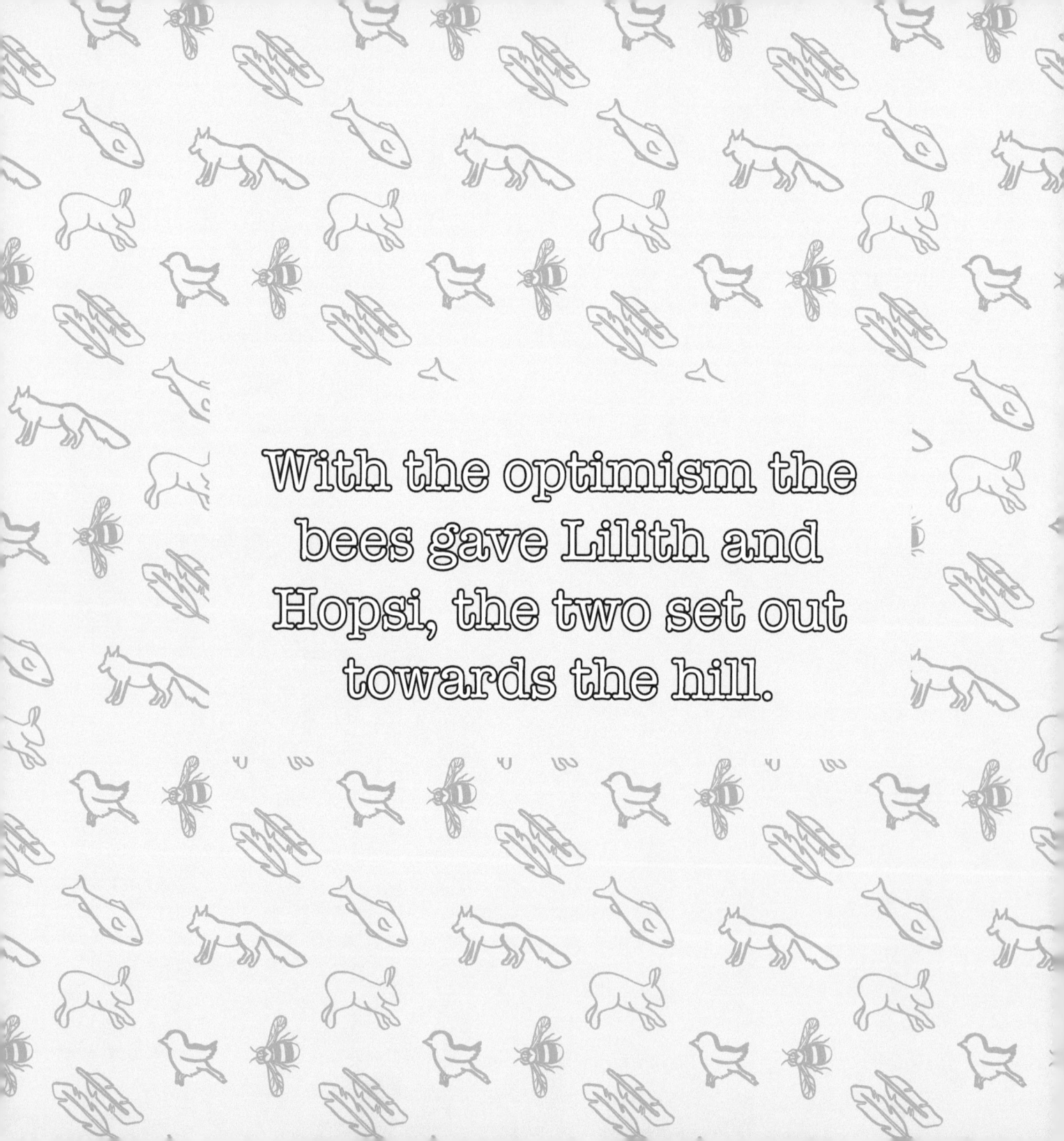

With the optimism the bees gave Lilith and Hopsi, the two set out towards the hill.

When they reached the base of the hill, the two enjoyed a snack Hopsi had packed. They felt nourished and strong. With tiny steps they reached the top of the hill.

It wasn't long before a very large animal came wandering towards them on the same path. A bear with thick brown hair.

With a rough growly voice, Berry the bear said, "You two look lost, can I help you find something?"

Hopsi replied with excitement, "Oh Berry, you're so kind. Yes you can help us. Help us get to the moon!"

Berry opened his gentle eyes wide and said, "If I were you, I would travel in that direction. I always find things, good things in that direction." Berry pointed with his massive paw towards the mountain. "Sorry that I cannot help more, I ate too many berries and can't stop tooting."

"Thank you Berry," replied Hopsi, "We better start moving. Soon it will be night and soon we will reach the moon!" So the two little friends set out on their way towards the mountain.

Berry also warned them that the moon might be roaming, trying to find them. That didn't stop them, the two little ones traveled on their way.

The sun was setting. The sky was clear. The wind lay still and the sounds of the day were fading. With easy steps, they made it to the mountain.

Hopsi and Lilith came to a halt when they heard rocks falling. They looked up. There stood deer. Hopsi said, "Dearest Doe, we seek the moon, how far are we?" Doe replied, "Small walkers, you've almost made it. Although I've never been, I know that you're not too far. Go to the mountain lake, the lake will take you there. Sorry that I cannot help more, I must find better grazing pastures and gardens."

Lilith and Hopsi expressed their gratitude to Doe and continued onward in search for the moon. They moved towards the mountain lake.

Doe also warned them to be
cautious of the moon. That
didn't stop them,
the two little ones traveled
on their way.

It wasn't long before they came across crystal clear water. They peered into the water and saw uncountable fish. Fishes of all colors and sizes. A trout sprung out from the water and caught a bug. Then sprung up again and said, "Look, look behind you!"

Lilith and Hopsi turned their bodies around. There before them was a wolf with fur like silver. The wolf was one of the more mysterious creatures of the forest. Wolf was so stunning that the two little explorers didn't know how to react. They had never encountered such an animal.

With a calm soothing voice the wolf said, "Hello, my name is Luna. I've followed you throughout your journey to the moon."

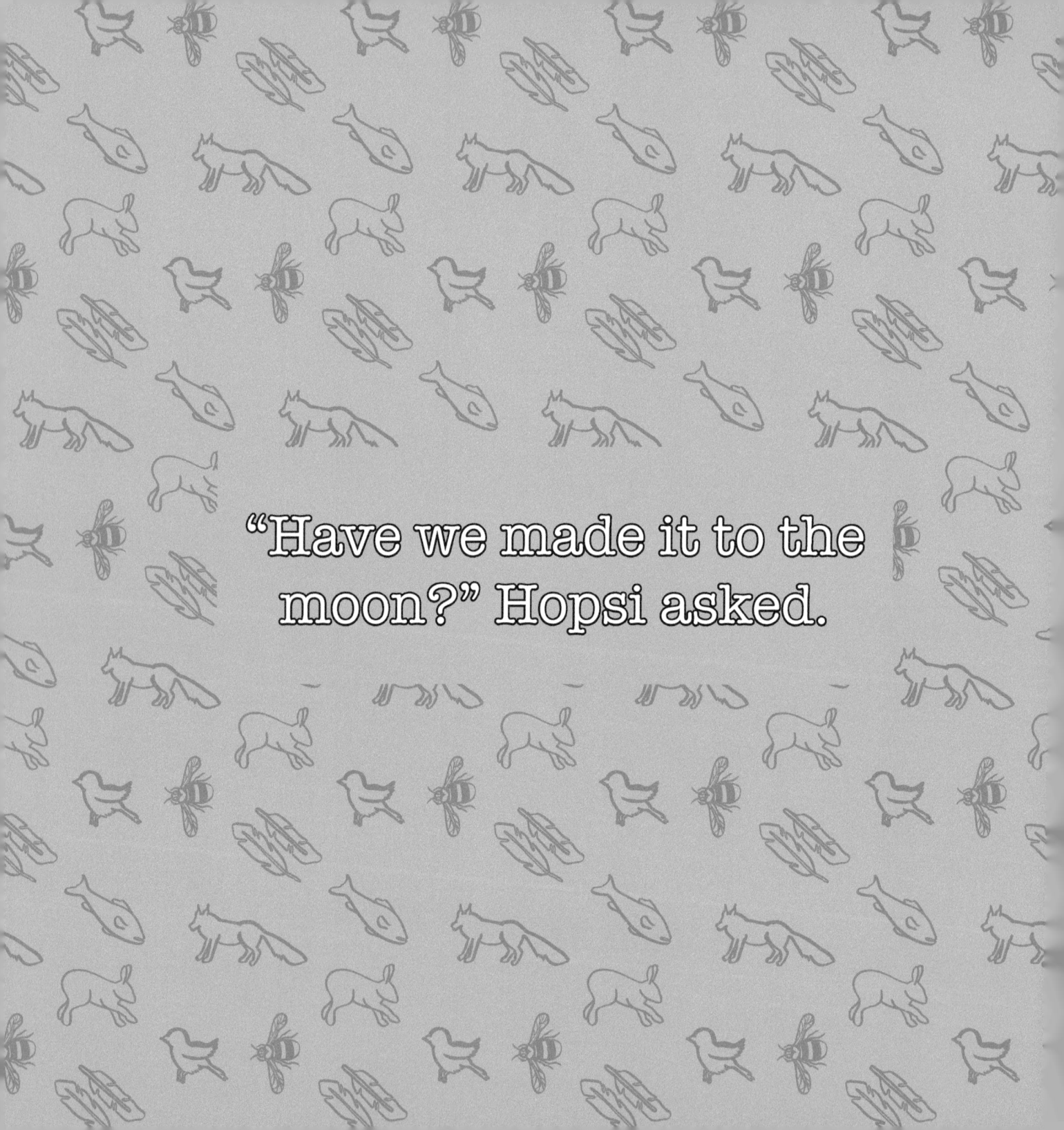

"Have we made it to the moon?" Hopsi asked.

Luna replied, "The animals you encountered on your travels know me as the moon and they have directed you to me.

"I can guide you to the moon you're looking for," said Luna, "I've been traveling with you from the beginning."

"From the yard of your home. To the bird in the trees. To the fox at the edge of the woods. To the bees in the flower field. To the bear on the hill. To the deer on the mountain. To the trout in the mountain lake. Here I am to help you find the moon. Your small feet have gone far enough today."

Hopsi and Lilith realized that night had fallen. The stars spread across the dark blue sky like glitter confetti. Luna said, "Look there, you've made it!"

Lilith and Hopsi gazed into the reflection of the mountain lake. The two little ones had found what they were seeking that day. There was the moon, fabulously glowing, big and bright, right before their eyes.

As they gazed at the mysterious and majestic moon, Lilith and Hopsi knew from then on that they could accomplish anything as long as they had one another.

Also, with a little help
from their friends.

END

> Great things are done by a series
> of small things brought together.
> ~ Vincent Van Gogh

Contributor Credits:

Irene Lovejoy, Vivian Stuck, Ben Carter, Rhylee Smith, Catherine Coleman, Mary and Stuart Lovejoy, Susan Stuck, Heather Hardy, Kathy and Bill Gourlie, Savanna Davenport, Cassandra Kane, Emily Bulfin and Jalal Jemison, Sarah Kiley, Lia Harch, Torie Nguyen, Lizabeth Ralles, Rupa Raman and Kartik Royapet, Don Gourlie, Robert Truman, Diana Hirshfeld, Robb N. Johnston, Stephanie Dutka, Aaron Lovejoy, Erin Hunt, Todd Mooney, Dennis Thompson, James Dillon Bennett, Kristin Arnold, Richard Zahniser, Lynn Bousquet, Laura LJ Alcantara, Sara Jean, Lucy Salinas, Sam Baraso, Justyn Buske, Emily Reede, Nathan Beird, Ben Levinson, Leah Sawick, John B. McCarthy, David Miller, Nic Justice, Christine Heaney, Rebecca Addy, Danny Mendoza, Ryan Read, Nathan Kohrmann, Maarten Leo Daalder, Andrey Novoseltsev, Elizabeth Karr, Oliver O'Brien, Leslie McClure, Geetha Raman, Carla DiGennaro, Sarah Kiley, Brandon Avery, Stoney Bennett, Emilie Abourizk, Pam Rabeck, Jamie Nelsen, Jacob Conner Kear, Indu Rajan, Katie Stuck Anderson, Debbie Stone Hobbs, Siri Basak, Tess Baker, Cindi Earl Bratvold, Ashley Byma, Catherine Leja, Karen McKibben, Ashley Joy, Zach Honey, Lisa Poe, Alyssa Wetzsteon, Whitney Phillips, James D, Angela Simmons, Tracee Danyluk, Danielle Fuchs, Stephanie Newman, Diane Byrnes, Hannah Honey, Christina, Che Broadnax, Amy Bargfrede, John Davenport, Patty and Ross McCallister, Anita Witta, Jessica Loomis and Brian Barnes, Erica Strachan, Carolina Ciappa, William Kolski, Jason Williams, Aaron Lebowitz, Kate Rountree

Contributor Dedications:
-To Matilda, love Mom
-To Dakota, Savannah & Rocky, love Rhylee Smith
- To my 3 granddaughters, love Cindi Earl Bratvold
- To Kennedy Rose Becker, love Debbie Stone Hobbs
- To Margaret, love Mommy & Daddy
- To Stella, love Mom & Dad

www.ingramcontent.com/pod-product-compliance
Lightning Source LLC
Chambersburg PA
CBHW041721240626
47171CB00003B/21